Printed 2022

Wonder House

(An imprint of Prakash Books Pvt. Ltd.)

First published in India in 2021

Wonder House Books

Corporate & Editorial Office

113-A, 1st Floor, Ansari Road, Daryaganj, New Delhi-110002

Tel +91 11 2324 7062-65

ISBN : 9789354401824

Illustrated & Written by
Ishan Trivedi

Editors
Manpreet Kaur Aden
Aadithyan Mohan K.
Gurbani Kaur
Raina Guglani

Designers
Payal Jaipuria
Neeraj Sharma

Printed in India

ROYAL SECRETS

Illustrated & Written by Ishan Trivedi

Wonder House

There once lived a glorious king and a charming queen,

She always covered her face with a veil, so it was never seen.

The king wore a big, bright turban,

And they cared for all under the Sun.

The king built a golden pavilion for the queen in their castle's gardens,

There the queen spent her days, singing and dancing with her maidens.

Many lotuses bloomed in
the garden pond,

Where several small and
beautiful fish were found.

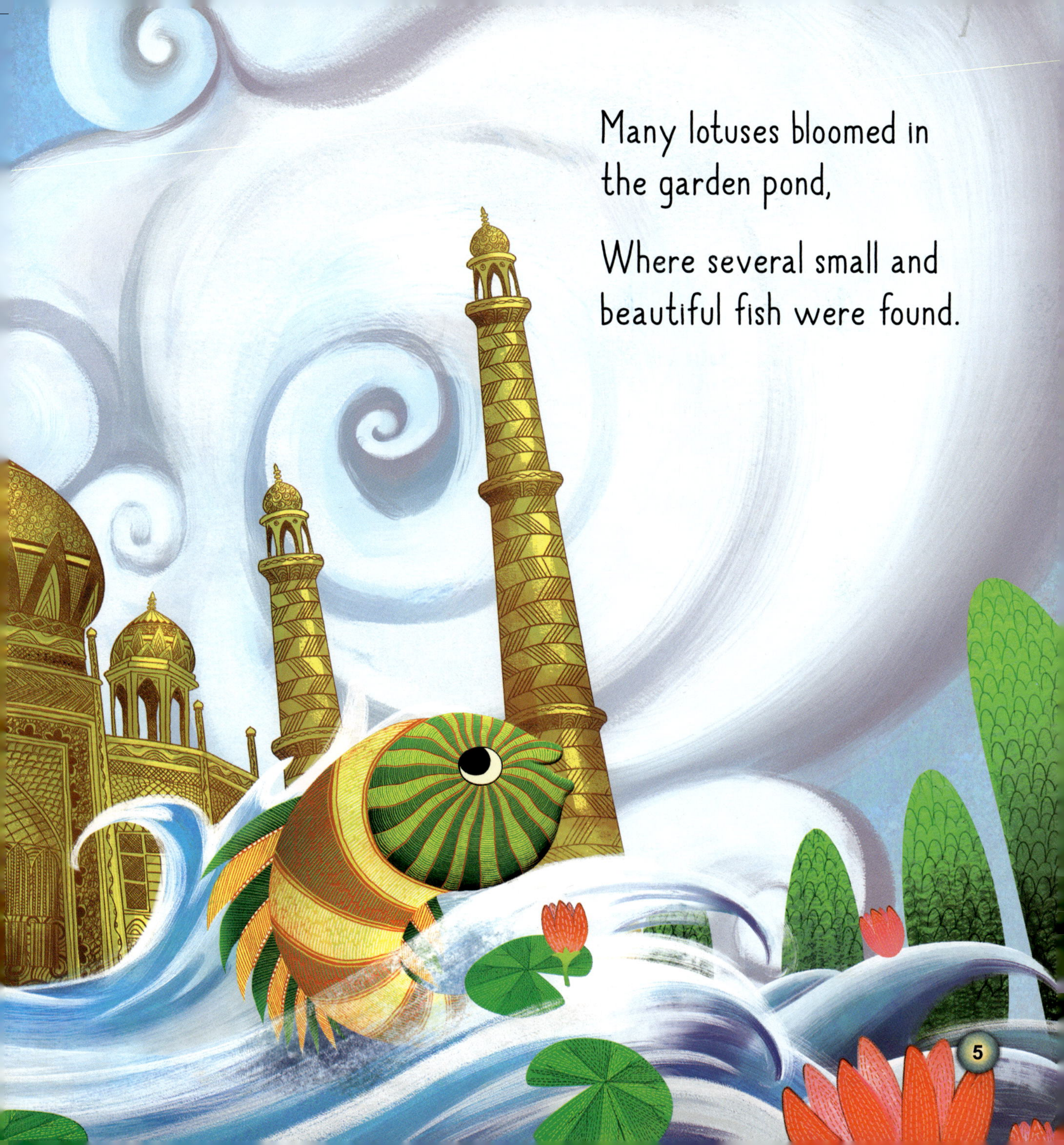

One fine evening as the queen danced around the pond in bliss,

She suddenly slipped into the water and frightened a fish.

Afraid but curious, the fish took a glance,

They saw the queen's charming face by chance!

The queen's long hidden secret came into sight,
The fish saw she had a squint in the watery light!
Ashamed, she threatened them to keep their lips sealed,
Unless they wanted to be imprisoned and heeled.

The next day, full of the secret, the fish started bloating up.

They found this knowledge indigestible and started floating up!

Soon, they were soaring around the sky,

Shocked by this scaly balloon, a bird came flying by.

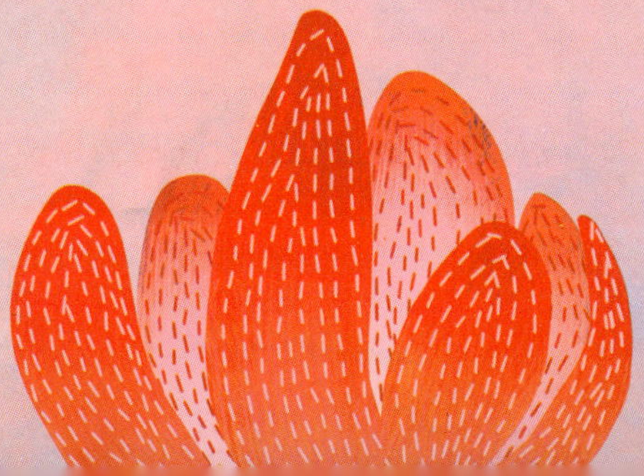

The bird asked the fish if they were unwell,
Or under any kind of strange spell.
And if they are feeling stressed,
The matter needs to be addressed.

Feeling exhausted, the fish let the truth out,
Upon hearing which the bird grew stout.
Promising to tell no one in town,
The bird watched the fish sink down.

The bird tried to keep moving on,
But they felt heavy and moved like a pawn,
As the secret swelled up inside their head,
Clouding up their mind with knowledge unsaid.

A hunter down the road saw the odd bird,

It was interesting, fluffy, and absurd!

He knew his family would laugh and smile,

So he set up a trap with amazing style!

He lured in the bird to his woven net,
And the bird and captivity immediately met!
He asked them how they got so much fluff,
And the bird was feeling too full to try and bluff.

The bird had to reveal the secret to the hunter,
They started blowing it out, leaving him to ponder,
As they felt uplifted and asked him not to tell,
They rose up into the sky, wishing him well.

Later that night, the hunter returned to his home.
His wife was shocked at his belly–round like a dome!
She asked if there was anything he wanted to tell?
She said "If you have done something, I won't yell."

The hunter cried. He was bound by a promise,
His wife convinced him to stop being so modest.
She stated that you should not hide anything from your wife.
At last, he told her the secret so he could have a happy life.

For the wife, the secret was getting hard to digest,

Her stomach kept bloating, making it odd for her to rest.

She went out to fetch water from the well.

Her friends asked her the reason for looking so unwell.

She couldn't stop herself from spilling the secret to her friends.

She asked them all to swear not to share it with anyone else!

The secret was no more a secret,

which led people to enquire.

The rumor soon started to spread like a fire.

Now the rumor was out and wide,
the minister decided to inform the king
that they can no longer hide.

When the minister told the king,

he was left surprised.

The queen heard it all,

and ran away to hide.

As the secret got exposed,
people began to sing.

If the queen is not beautiful,
She is not suitable for our king.

The king wanted to see his queen,
and searched for her everywhere.
The queen was in hiding,
and could not be found anywhere.
Not in the castle, nowhere in the garden.
He got stressed from being uncertain.
He remembered the queen loves to read
whenever she is tense.
He knew right away where she went.

Knowing this he ran to the books,
In the library she would sit in some nook.
He saw her behind a pile in tears,
And asked her if he could come near.

hrough her sobs he gave his confession,
My queen, I have my own deception."
I am sure you will leave me, my dear,
Vhen you learn that I have monkey ears!"

What is a king without his queen?

Let's promise each other,

no more secrets in between.

Nobody is and can be perfect.

We should love our uniqueness
and accept ourselves.

Then together in their joy
they did many things,

Secure in their love, where
it all begins.